Tom and the Tree House

This book belongs.

too

<u>Daniel paydar</u>

Tom and the Tree House

Joan Lingard

Catnip

CATNIP BOOKS
Published by Catnip Publishing Ltd
Quality Court, off Chancery Lane
London WC2A 1HR

This edition first published 2013
1 3 5 7 9 10 8 6 4 2

First published in Great Britain in 1998 by Hodder Children's Books.

Cover illustration by Steven Wood
Cover design by Pip Johnson

A CIP catalogue record for this book is available from the British
Library.

ISBN 978-1-84647-172-8

Printed and bound by CPI Group (UK) Ltd, Croydon, CR0 4YY

www.catnippublishing.co.uk

For Rosa and Aedan
with love

Chapter One

Tom knew he was adopted. He had always known, ever since he could remember. His parents, the ones who had adopted him, Helen and Mike Watson, had made no secret of it. They had told him even before he could properly understand.

They talked to him about it when he was five, and going to school for the first time.

'You weren't born to us, Tom. We

chose you. So you're very special. Not every child is chosen.'

For a while Tom went around feeling special. He looked at new babies in their prams and he thought, 'You're not special. Your mum and dad didn't choose you.'

He said to his friend Sam Flynn, 'I'm special, but you're not.'

'How not?' demanded Sam, sucking noisily through a straw.

They were in Sam's room, drinking juice and eating carrot cake made by Sam's mother. She baked a lot of cakes, of all kinds. Chocolate, jam and cream sponge, banana. Mrs Flynn was at home all day, whereas Tom's mother went out to work and had no time to make cakes.

Mrs Flynn was a childminder. She collected Tom from school with Sam

every day and brought him home until
his own mother got back from work.

'You can't be special, can you?' said
Tom. "Cos your mum and dad didn't
choose you. They had to take you
whether they wanted to or not.'

Sam frowned.

'Mine didn't have to take me,' said Tom. 'They chose me. So I'm special.'

This worried Sam, who told his parents what Tom had said when he was getting ready for bed that night.

'Of course you're special!' said Mrs Flynn, giving him a hug.

'But Tom says you had to take me whether you wanted to or not.'

'That's silly!' said Mr Flynn.

'If you hadn't liked me would you still have taken me?' asked Sam. Would they have left him on the doorstep for people like Mr and Mrs Watson to come along and choose?

'Of course we would have taken you,' said Mr Flynn. 'Anyway, we liked you from the moment we set eyes on you.'

'You are very special because you are our child,' said Mrs Flynn. 'You were born to us and no one else.'

'Tom wasn't as lucky as you,' said Mr Flynn. 'His mother couldn't keep him so she had to have him adopted. But he's very lucky that it was the Watsons who adopted him.'

Next day, Sam said to Tom, 'Your mum didn't want you. Not your real one. My dad says you're lucky that Mr and Mrs Watson took you in. You might have been left lying on the doorstep of a hospital if they hadn't.'

Tom didn't feel special any longer. When he went home he brooded on what Sam had said. While his mother was cooking the supper he went out into the backyard. His father was away for the night. He was a sales representative and sold gas- and oil-fired boilers to people all over the country, so he was often away.

Tom kicked a large jaggy stone round the yard. He stubbed his toe and hopped about on one foot for a bit. Then he started kicking again. He ended up hitting  Percy the cat, who yelped as if he'd been struck by lightning and leapt on to the kitchen window sill. He always knew how to make the most of things!

Out came Mrs Watson.

'Don't do that, Tom love! You'll hurt poor old Percy. He's not as young as he used to be.'

'If he dies you can always adopt another cat.'

Mrs Watson, his unreal mother, looked at him. 'What's the matter, Tom?'

She came over and tried to put her arm round him, but he moved away from her.

'Sam says I'm not special at all!'

'But you are!'

'If I was so special why did my mum – my *real* mum – give me away? She couldn't have liked me.'

'Let's go inside, love.'

They went inside.

'Come and sit beside me.' Mrs Watson patted the sofa.

Tom sat down, leaving a gap between them.

Percy came padding in. He gave Tom a dirty look and bounded on to Mrs Watson's knee. She fondled his ears. He closed his eyes and purred, making a noise like an oil-fired boiler.

'Your mum was very young when she had you, Tom,' said Mrs Watson.

'And she didn't have enough money to keep you.'

'How old was she?' Tom scratched his knee. He had a scab that was almost healed. He began to pick at it.

Mrs Watson didn't seem to want to tell him.

'How old?' he asked again. He had his nail under the edge of the scab. It was tempting to lift it up. When he tried to he felt the skin underneath pucker.

'Sixteen. That's very young for a girl to take care of a baby.'

'She couldn't have loved me.' His knee was smarting where his finger was poking.

'I'm sure she did.'

'How do you know? Did you ask her?'

'No. We never met her. But she

wanted the best for you, Tom. That's why she gave you to us for adoption.'

'I don't call that a very good reason.' He bent over to see what was happening to his knee. A trickle of bright blood was emerging from the side of the crusty brown scab.

'It's the best reason. She thought of your happiness before her own.'

He had a good hold of the scab now. With a quick yank he ripped it off. The pain made him catch his breath, but he stopped himself from crying. Blood spurted from his knee and ran down into his socks.

'Now look what you've done!' cried his unreal mother, and Percy sprang up from her knee and vaulted on to the floor.

Mrs Watson fetched warm water and

Dettol and cotton wool. Tom put his
leg up on the sofa and she bathed the
wound carefully, trying not to make it

smart even more. He bit hard on his bottom lip.

'I've told you not to keep picking the scab!' she said, but she didn't sound properly cross. 'It will never mend otherwise. And you don't want a scar on your knee for the rest of your life, do you?'

He didn't know if he would mind or not.

She put a clean dressing and a large plaster on his knee and told him to sit where he was until supper was ready. He must rest the leg so that the blood would stop flowing.

'I'll put the television on.'

It was time for the children's programmes. Tom was glad to lie back and watch television. He was tired after a day in school, and all that arguing with Sam.

For a long time he forgot about being special or not special. He didn't really think about it properly again until his eighth birthday.

Chapter Two

Tom wanted a dog for his birthday. Sam had got a puppy for his birthday the month before, a beautiful, silky golden-haired Labrador. Sam was over the moon. He'd called him Goldie.

The boys took Goldie to the park. There, they could let him off his lead. He was a frisky puppy and strong for his size and they often had to run to keep up with him. He jumped up and down, muddying their fronts with his

19

paws, but they didn't mind. He licked their hands. He barked excitedly. He was a lot of fun.

Tom liked going for walks with Sam and Goldie, except that when they had to put the puppy on the lead Sam wouldn't let him have a turn. Sam held on to it determinedly.

'He's my dog,' he said. 'Why don't you ask your mum and dad if you can get one of your own? For your birthday. And then we can take them for walks together.'

Tom asked his parents.

'I'm afraid we couldn't have a dog, Tom,' said his father sadly. 'You can't leave a dog on its own all day. It's different for a cat. They're much more independent.'

Percy glanced up from washing his hind legs and gave a superior grin as if he had understood. Tom wouldn't have been one bit surprised if he had!

'Mrs Flynn doesn't go out to work,' said Tom's mother. 'So there's someone in their house all the time.'

'I wish you didn't have to go out to work,' said Tom.

'We need the money, I'm afraid. And, besides, I like my job. I think it's important.'

She worked in a laboratory that did medical research.

'Your mum's work helps save people's lives,' said his father.

'I still wish she didn't have to work, though,' said Tom. 'And then I could have a puppy. It's not fair!'

'Not everyone can have the same things in life, Tom,' said his mother.

'But we will get you something very nice for your birthday,' said his father. 'Don't worry.'

He didn't want something 'very nice'. He wanted a puppy, which would be the nicest thing of all.

On the morning of his birthday, he woke up thinking about a dog. He crossed his fingers for luck. You never know, they might have changed their minds!

He went downstairs. A very large, wrapped parcel was propped up against the sofa. It obviously wasn't a dog. It was too large and knobbly looking.

'Happy birthday, dear Tom,' sang

his parents. 'Happy birthday to you.'

'Aren't you going to open your present?' asked his father.

Tom tore off the wrapping paper. He knew before he'd finished that it was going to be a bicycle. He could feel the handlebars and the pedals jutting out.

'So what do you think?' His mother was smiling.

It was a very nice bicycle, Tom had to admit, and his old one was getting too small for him.

'Fantastic!' he said, quickly forgetting all about a dog. 'Thanks, Mum! Thanks, Dad!' He hugged each of them in turn.

His birthday had fallen on a Saturday, which was very convenient since his father was at home and Tom himself didn't have to go to school. Sam was coming to tea. Mrs Watson baked a very fine chocolate cake and decorated it with smarties and eight candles.

When Sam arrived he had Goldie with him.

'He doesn't like it when I leave him behind,' he explained. 'He yelps at the back of the door waiting for me to come back. But he'll be very good.'

Mrs Watson was looking dubious. 'We'll need to put Percy out.'

Percy had vaulted on to the top of the kitchen cupboard from where he was regarding Goldie with a murderous eye. The puppy was barking excitedly.

'It's all right, Goldie,' said Sam. 'Percy won't eat you.'

'He would if he got the chance,' said Tom.

At that moment Percy came plummeting down, snarling and spitting, with his claws extended. He landed on Goldie's back.

The next few minutes were hectic while Mr Watson tried to separate the two animals. Sam panicked and the puppy yelped and ran in circles and Percy continued to hiss and try to scratch his eyes out. He went on hissing and struggling even after Mr Watson had seized him by the scruff of the neck and was carrying him out into the garden.

'You shouldn't have brought Goldie,' said Tom to Sam. 'This is Percy's place and he doesn't like other animals coming into it.'

'Just as well you didn't get a puppy for your birthday then, isn't it?' said Sam.

'Well, never mind all that now!' said Mrs Watson, keen to change the subject. 'Percy can quite easily stay outside.'

When Mr Watson came back he had a nasty scratch on his hand which his wife had to treat with Dettol.

'Now let's have tea!' she said brightly, putting the bottle back on its shelf.

Throughout tea Percy sat on the dining room window sill, glaring in at them with his green eyes. Whenever Goldie moved he got up and arched his back.

'Ignore him,' said Mr Watson.

They had a good tea, except that Mrs Watson didn't eat very much. Tom noticed that she looked pale but when he asked her if she was all right she said she was fine. Mr Watson kept glancing anxiously at her too.

Tom blew out his candles in one puff and made a wish.

'I bet I know what you wished,' said Sam.

'Bet you don't!' retorted Tom, but Sam probably had guessed.

'Cake, boys?' Mrs Watson held out the plate.

They had two pieces of chocolate cake apiece.

'That was good cake,' said Sam.

Mrs Watson was pleased since Sam's mother had such a high reputation as a cake-maker.

The boys went upstairs to play as the garden wouldn't be safe for Goldie.

'Shall we play Cluedo?' suggested Tom.

But as soon as they started to put the pieces out on the board Goldie jumped on it messing everything up. Then he found one of Tom's slippers and took it under the bed.

'He's chewing it!' cried Tom.

By the time they got Goldie

out from under the bed he'd chewed a hole in the toe.

'Nothing's safe with a dog around,' said Sam cheerfully.

They played a computer game for a while since Goldie couldn't do anything to that, then it was time for Sam to go home.

'I'll go down the road with you,' said Tom, 'on my bike.'

Sam thanked Mrs Watson for the tea and put a lead on Goldie.

Tom cycled slowly beside them.

'It's a great bike,' he said. 'It's got twelve gears.'

Sam's bike only had six.

'Don't suppose you need twelve very often,' said Sam.

'If you go for long runs you might.' said Tom. 'My dad's going to take me for a cycling weekend. We're going to camp. You can't do that unless you've got a bike like this. I'm glad I got this instead of a dog.'

'I'm glad I got Goldie,' said Sam.

They parted at Sam's gate and Tom cycled home. He hadn't told the whole truth of course when he'd said he'd rather have the bike instead of a dog. But he wasn't going to let Sam Flynn know that!

When he got home his mother was being sick in the bathroom.

'What's wrong with Mum?' he cried.

 He'd heard her being sick before, in the mornings before he got up. He was afraid she might have some terrible disease. 'Is she ill, Dad?'

She came out of the bathroom.

'I think we're going to have to tell him now, Mike, don't you?' she said to her husband.

'Tell me what?' said Tom.

'We're going to have a baby,' said Mrs Watson.

Chapter Three

'You mean you're going to adopt another baby?' said Tom.

'Well, no,' said Mrs Watson. She hesitated before going on. 'Tom, I'm pregnant. That's why I've been feeling sick. But that will pass and then I'll feel great again.'

Tom didn't feel great. He felt stupid. Real dumb-head stupid. He was trying to take in what she'd said. They'd always told him they couldn't have a baby of their own. That was why they'd adopted him.

'But you said—'

'I know,' said Mr Watson. 'We thought we couldn't have a baby, but now after all these years we've found that we can.'

'It's a bit like a miracle, really,' said Mrs Watson.

She smiled at her husband and he smiled back at her. You could see that they couldn't help smiling.

'I expect you're glad you're going to have a baby of your own,' muttered Tom.

'It'll be your baby, too, though, Tom,' said Mrs Watson.

Tom backed away so that she couldn't hug him. He didn't want to be touched.

'Don't you think it might be rather nice to have a brother or a sister?' said Mr Watson. 'Not to be an only child any longer?'

Sam had two brothers and a sister. He had to share his bedroom with his younger brother and they were always fighting. Sam's brother kept taking his things and messing them up.

'Will I have to share my room with it?' asked Tom.

'No question of that,' said Mr Watson. 'I'm going to do up the spare room as a nursery.'

From then on the baby seemed to take over the house, long before it was even born.

The spare room, which had always been full of junk, was cleared out and most of the stuff stored in the garden shed. You could hardly get the door of the shed open now. Tom had to keep his bike in the porch.

Mr Watson had to do the decorating of the spare room at weekends. He wouldn't let his wife help in any way. She wasn't allowed to stand on ladders and stretch.

'You have to take care of yourself, Helen!' he said. 'We may not get another chance.'

He meant to have a baby, Tom knew that. Nearly everything that was said was about the baby. They kept telling him what he'd be able to do with it.

'You can help to bath him, Tom!' Or take her out in the pushchair or play with her in the garden or read to him. Sometimes they called the baby 'him' and sometimes 'her'. Tom always thought of it as 'it'.

Mr Watson painted the baby's ceiling blue and put gold stars on it. They went – the three of them – to the decorating shop to choose the wallpaper. Tom would rather have gone to play with Sam and Goldie, but his parents said they would like him to come with them.

'We want you to help us choose,' said Mr Watson.

They thumbed through books of boring old wallpaper.

'What do you think, Tom?' asked Mrs Watson. 'Shall we have the blue and yellow paper with the teddies or the blue and white one with the clowns?'

Tom pointed to another one that was mostly orange, black and white, and had tigers strewn across it.

'I don't think that would be a good idea!' laughed Mrs Watson. 'It might frighten him. When he's bigger maybe. But not when he's a baby.'

They chose the yucky teddies.

'We'll do something together next weekend, Tom,' promised Mr Watson.

But when next weekend came he had time only for a quick, half-hour cycle run with Tom. He had too many other things to do. Like hang up curtains to match the teddy wallpaper and lay a blue, fitted carpet.

'You were going to take me camping, Dad,' Tom reminded him.

'I know! And I will. It's just I'm so pushed for time, with being away all week.'

On Monday morning, Mr Watson went off as usual.

In school that day Tom thought about his parents and the baby. It would be their real child. All that rubbish they'd given him about being special! He'd believed them because he'd been younger then. But what could be more special than being the real child of your parents?

At suppertime, he wasn't very hungry.

'What's on your mind, Tom?' asked Mrs Watson softly. 'Tell me!'

'I was just wondering what my mum was called?' He had not thought to ask before. 'The other one. You know.'

'Who gave birth to you? She was called Louise.'

'Where does she live?'

'I don't know, love, really I don't.'

'You wouldn't tell me if you did though, would you?'

'Probably not.'

'Why not? Would you not want me to go looking for her?'

'When you're older that would be all right, but it wouldn't do you any good at the moment. Or her, either. Or us. All our lives would be upset.'

'She might change her mind and have me back.'

'That's not possible, Tom. And we couldn't bear to part with you! You're our son, and we love you. You know that, don't you?'

'Yes,' he muttered, without looking her in the eye. He did know they loved him, but his real mum might love him just as much, mightn't she? Or even more? Enough to let him have a dog.

'Dad was thinking of redecorating your room,' said Mrs Watson, 'now that he's more or less finished the nursery. Would you like that? You could choose the colours and we might stretch to a new downie!'

Tom shrugged.

Next day, a white-painted chest of drawers was delivered to the house. Then came a basket lined with white, and a tiny quilted yellow eiderdown edged with lace. Gradually the baby's room filled up with baths and changing mats and packets of nappies and jars of ointment and talcum powder and funny looking garments called baby-grows. When each object was brought in Tom was called to admire it.

Finally, the room had everything in it that a new baby could want.

'So what do you think, Tom?' asked Mrs Watson.

'I think I'm going to build a tree house,' he said.

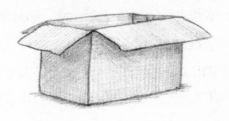

Chapter Four

They had a large garden with well-grown trees and shrubs, protected by a high stone wall. By the back wall there was a big old oak tree. It was good for climbing since it had plenty of footholds. The branches started low down and were thick and well spread.

This was the tree that Tom chose for his house. He began work on it straight away. He rummaged about in the shed and managed to unearth a large cardboard box. It was the one they'd brought their new television set home in.

He dragged the box up the tree and placed it in the broadest fork, turning it on its side so that the open part faced the garden.

'Maybe you should try to anchor it down,' suggested Mrs Watson, who was watching anxiously below.

She found some rope and threw it up to him. He had a job lashing it over the top of the box and the surrounding branches. Trying to do that and keep his balance at the same time wasn't easy. His foot slipped a couple of times.

'Careful!' called Mrs Watson, before going back into the house.

Tom was hot and sticky by the time he had more or less managed to secure the box in position. It still looked a bit lopsided, but it would have to do, for now.

He eased himself inside his cardboard house. There was just room for him to sit. The box rocked a little and he had to be careful not to move.

He thought about Louise. His real

mother. She would be twenty-four now, he reckoned, or twenty-five. That was much younger than Mrs Watson, who was forty. He pictured her with long, smooth, blond hair and brown, smiley eyes. His hair was fair, and his eyes brown. Children usually looked like their parents, didn't they? Sam had flaming red hair, the same as his dad.

'Lou-ise.' Tom tried the name on his tongue. He said it softly, like a whisper. It was a nice name, a soft sounding name. Her voice would be soft and gentle, like her smile. He was going to keep a look out for her. Chances were she might live nearby. He was sure he would recognise her. Anyone would know their own mother, wouldn't they?

It was nice being up here, tucked away, high above the garden, looking down. This was a place of his own where he

could think about Louise. Mrs Watson might not like him to think about his real mother in her house.

Soon he was called in for supper. After he had climbed down from the tree he turned back to look at it. 'It's all squint,' he said crossly. 'It's a mess!'

'It's not so easy building a house, is it?' said Mrs Watson.

It rained that night. Heavily. In the morning, water was still dripping from the gutters. Percy came in from his early morning prowl with his coat drenched.

Tom ran outside to look at his tree house. The cardboard was all soggy and the top had caved in. It was a sorry looking sight! 'It's ruined!' he said in disgust.

He took it down and squashed up the wet mess. He stamped on it, then he threw it in the big garden bin.

'Maybe it's just as well,' said Mrs Watson. 'We didn't want you falling out of it, did we? And breaking your neck!'

He didn't mention the tree house to Sam on the way to school. Sam would just say something like, 'Any twit would know better than to make a house out of cardboard!'

There was a buzz of excitement in

their classroom that morning. Their teacher had gone off to have a baby – was everyone having a baby? – and they were getting a supply teacher until she came back.

The headmistress brought the new teacher in and introduced her.

'Boys and girls, this is Miss Farrow. I want you to be on your very best behaviour and help her in every way you can.'

Miss Farrow was young and pretty. She had brown eyes that made Tom think of pansies and her blond hair was cut round her ears in a bob.

The girls were soon tripping over themselves to help.

Yes, Miss Farrow! No, Miss Farrow! Can I get you a glass of water? A new stick of chalk? Can I water the crocus bulbs for you? Carry your bag?

The boys sat back, not making any move to help, but they didn't make any fusses, either. In the playground it was generally agreed that Miss Farrow was okay, as teachers went.

After school, as Sam and Tom were leaving the room, another teacher looked in.

'Oh, there you are, Louise!' she said to the supply teacher.

Chapter Five

Tom stumbled out into the corridor in a daze.

'Did you hear what she said? She called her Louise.'

'So what?' said Sam. 'Lots of people are called Louise.'

'Not lots,' said Tom.

'My cousin is.'

'That doesn't prove anything.'

Sam wasn't interested in talking about it any more. He wanted to get home and take Goldie out.

'You never want to do anything but take Goldie out these days,' complained Tom.

'You're just jealous,' said Sam.

'Am not!' said Tom.

He could go straight home after school now that Mrs Watson had started her maternity leave. She was stopping work for six months.

When Tom got home he had a drink of juice and a piece of banana bread, then he went out into the garden. He climbed the oak tree and sat in the fork, his fork. He thought about Miss Farrow. Louise.

She had blond hair and brown eyes. And she must be about twenty-five years old. Also, she must live somewhere not too far away. So she could be, couldn't she, she just could be . . . ? His mother!

It was an amazing thought and he felt amazed by it. He sat there for a long time, until the cold forced him down.

'It was time you came in!' said Mrs Watson.

'Did my mum call me Tom?' he asked. 'Or did you?'

'We did.'

That disappointed him. If his mother had given him his name she might have been keeping an eye open for a boy of eight and a half with blond hair and brown eyes called Tom.

'I'm going to start on a new tree house,' he said.

'I thought you'd given up the idea?'

'This time it's going to be a proper house, not one made of silly old cardboard. When Dad comes home I'm going to ask him to help me.'

Mr Watson was keen to help him.

'What we need is a wooden box!' he said. 'A good-sized wooden one. I can think of the very thing.'

On Saturday morning, they took the car and drove to the warehouse belonging to the firm that Mr Watson worked for. The foreman found them an old plywood container that had held an oil-fired boiler. It measured four by four by three feet.

'That's big!' said Tom. 'I'll be able to stand up in it.'

To get the box in the car they had to take it apart. They drove home with the boot lid propped open.

'First of all,' said Mr Watson, 'we have to lay some beams across the branches to make a base for the box.'

They looked in the shed to see what they could use for beams.

'These should fit the bill!' Mr Watson

hauled out several four by four inch old timber fence posts.

'It's a good thing you don't ever throw things out, isn't it, Dad?' said Tom.

'You'd better tell your mother that!'

They propped a long ladder against the oak tree, to make carrying materials up and down easier. They fitted the posts into the crook of the branches, then they lashed them to the branches of the tree with twine.

'We won't put nails into the tree,' said Mr Watson, 'as they would damage it.'

They were ready to lay the floor. They brought up the first piece of wood. Tom held a fistful of nails and passed them over one at a time to Mr Watson, who hammered them through the wood into the beams underneath.

'There!' he said, testing it. 'That seems steady enough. Now for the walls!'

He nailed the three walls into position, leaving an opening at the front for the door. After that, came the roof.

'Brilliant!' declared Tom.

They fitted a sheet of polythene over the top of the house, securing it with tacks, to keep the rain out. By this time it was almost dark. Mr Watson said he would help Tom make a door from the remaining piece of plywood next weekend.

'In the meantime you can get on and decorate your house!'

Tom did a bit each day. Mrs Watson gave him some dinosaur wallpaper that had been left over from his bedroom.

'It might be too much to put it all over such a small space,' she said. 'It could make you feel cramped.'

Tom thought about that and decided to put it on one wall only. He painted the other two walls a soft yellow colour and the ceiling white with emulsion paint from the shed.

Now for the floor.

In the shed there were various bits of old carpet. Tom chose a dark green piece.

'That will be in keeping with the tree and the garden,' said Mrs Watson.

She helped him to measure the floor and cut the carpet to size, using a sharp knife. He had to handle the knife very carefully. When he took the carpet up the ladder he found it fitted perfectly.

He was so pleased with his house that he decided to ask Sam to come and see it after all.

'You can't bring Goldie,' he told him.

'He might wreck the house and eat the carpet or piddle on it! Anyway, Goldie couldn't come into the garden because of Percy.

Sam stood on the top of the ladder and peered into Tom's house.

'It's a bit bare, isn't it?' he said.

'I've still got to furnish it,' said Tom. He was annoyed, though, with Sam. That was the last time he'd ask him up to his house! He felt sure if he were to ask Miss Farrow – Louise – to come and see it she would think it was lovely.

She was good at giving praise.

'That's very nice,' she would say when someone did a good drawing. 'I really like that.'

She smiled a lot. And laughed. As if she liked being with them. Tom watched her face when she talked or read a story. He liked the way she laughed and her cheeks dimpled. She had a bouncy laugh. It was the kind of laugh you'd like your mother to have. Even the boys were being helpful now, rushing to clean the blackboard and lay out fresh chalk.

'She's great, isn't she?' Tom said to Sam on their way home from school.

'Who?'

'Miss Farrow,' said Tom. He'd almost called her Louise! It was easy to think of her as Louise.

'She's all right,' said Sam. 'She gave me a row about my writing, though. She said it was messy.'

'Well, it is!'

'You're going all soppy over her!' said Sam accusingly. 'Teacher's pet!'

'I am not teacher's pet!' retorted Tom hotly.

He resolved never ever to mention her to Sam again.

After school each day he went straight to his tree house. He set about furnishing it. He took a large squashy orange cushion from his bedroom for something to sit on and in the shed came across an old wooden spool that would do for a table. It used to have electric cable coiled round it and was about a foot and a half across.

Now for something to keep his stuff on. He placed two bricks at either side of the back wall and laid a plank on top. That was just the job! He arranged his paperback books and toy cars on his new shelf.

'What about a travelling rug?' suggested Mrs Watson. 'To keep you warm on cold days.' She gave him an old green tartan one.

The temperature was warming up slightly. The snowdrops were out and the first of the crocuses. Mrs Watson picked some snowdrops and gave them to Tom for his house.

'Your house is beginning to get a lived-in look, Tom!' said Mr Watson when he came home.

He helped Tom make a door out of the remaining piece of plywood. They cut a rectangular hole for a window and covered it with perspex. Then they put hinges on the wood and fastened them to the sides of the house.

'Abracadabra!' said Mr Watson. 'We have a door!'

Mrs Watson gave Tom some plastic boxes in which to store biscuits and packets of crisps.

'The secret is to try and keep everything as dry as possible,' said Mr Watson. 'And leave the door open sometimes to air your house out.'

When the door was open Percy sneaked in. He liked sharpening his claws on the carpet. And from there he could keep a close eye on the birds.

The birds were gradually coming back. Thrushes built a nest in a sycamore tree next to the oak.

When the first of the young made their appearance Tom rushed inside to tell his parents.

'Come and see!' he cried. 'The thrushes are hatching!'

'Isn't that amazing?' said his dad. 'It seems we're about to do the same!'

Chapter Six

And so the baby was born. It was a 'her'.

Tom had to go and see it in hospital. His dad took him.

'This is Marigold, Tom,' said Mrs Watson, holding up a bundle wrapped tightly in a shawl. Only its face showed and some yellow fluff on the top of its head. 'Your little sister.'

'Her hair looks just like yours did when you were a baby,' said Mr Watson.

Tom knew that wasn't because she

was his real sister. He wondered if Louise had liked the colour of his hair when he was born.

'What do you think of her?' asked Mr Watson, who couldn't stop smiling. He meant the baby.

Tom started, for he'd still been thinking about Louise.

'Isn't she beautiful?' said Mrs Watson.

She didn't look beautiful to Tom. She had a red face that was wrinkled like a walnut and her eyelids were all puckered up.

'She looks a bit old,' he said, which made them laugh.

'She'll change,' said Mr Watson. 'You did!'

'We're glad she's a girl,' said Mrs Watson. 'So now we have a boy and a girl, the perfect family!'

She brought the baby home after a couple of days. Percy hid under the sofa when it yowled. Tom still thought of it as 'it.' He was astonished by how  loudly it could scream for one so small, and especially in the middle of the night. Mrs Watson had blue marks under her eyes and she yawned a lot.

'I'm not used to broken nights, Tom,' she said. 'You were a very good baby. You slept through the night from quite early on.'

The nights weren't the only thing that were broken. The whole house was in chaos. For the first week Mr Watson was on holiday and he sorted out the mess and did the washing. Then he had to go back to selling boilers.

'We've got to eat!' he said. 'It would be nice if you could give your mum a hand, Tom.'

When Tom came in from school the breakfast dishes were still lying in the sink and dirty baby clothes were scattered all over the bathroom floor. He had no intention of picking those smelly things up. He stepped over the top of them.

It was tidier in his tree house, and a lot quieter.

There was only the sound of the birds. He watched the male thrush flying to and fro bringing back insects and worms for the baby birds. He sat very still so as not to disturb them, except when Percy came on to the scene and had to shush them away. Percy knew the baby birds were up there and if he got the chance he'd snap one up. Mrs Watson said you couldn't blame him. He didn't know any better. That was just the way he was.

Tom was watching the birds when Mrs Watson came out to the back step with the baby held up against her. She had to wear a towel on her shoulder as it was always being sick.

'Tom!' she called. 'Do you want to come and help bath Marigold?'

She'd frightened the thrush. He had flown up into the air and was circling round the top of the tree flapping his wings.

'Please, Tom!' said Mrs Watson. 'I really could do with your help.'

'Oh, all right!' He slid down from the tree.

She asked him to help carry the bath into the living room where it would be warmer for Marigold.

'She's started to smile,' said Mrs Watson. 'Look, she's smiling at you.'

Tom didn't smile back. He stared hard at her but that didn't stop her smiling her gummy pink smile.

'You're very important to us, Tom, you know that, don't you?' said Mrs Watson. They were forever telling him so. 'You're our son.'

But not their real son. And he never could be.

After Marigold had been bathed and fed she went to sleep. So they were able to have a meal, Tom and his mum, just the two of them, with the baby in her basket on the kitchen counter. She slept throughout the meal.

'Fantastic!' said Mrs Watson. 'It's great to have a few minutes peace.'

Tom thought so, too.

'When will you be going back to work?' he asked.

'Marigold is much too young to leave!'

'I thought you'd be giving her to Mrs Flynn to mind?'

'Not this small.'

'When will you, then?'

'Tom, I've been meaning to tell you. I've given up my job.'

'Given it up?'

'Yes, I want to be with Marigold full-time while she's a baby. Maybe until she goes to school. I want to make the most of her. Also, I'm forty, and it's quite tiring at my age to have a new baby and go out to work.'

'You didn't give up work when you adopted me.'

'We needed the money then. And I was younger. I could cope.'

'And you wouldn't stay at home so that I could have a dog. It's only her you'll do it for! That's because she's your real child, isn't it?' shouted Tom.

He jumped up from the table, upsetting his juice. He ran out of the room, making for the garden. She followed him and caught hold of his arm before he could open the back door.

'Listen to me, Tom!' she cried, and then she said the same things over and over again, like how important he was and all that. But not as important as Marigold!

'You're every bit as important, Tom,' she said. 'You've got to believe me.'

But he couldn't.

He dreamt that night about his real mother. He couldn't see her face but he knew it was Miss Farrow.

The next day was the last day of term.

They were breaking up for the Easter holidays.

After school Tom let Sam go on ahead. He hung about in the classroom fiddling in his desk, waiting for everyone to leave. When they'd all gone he went up to Miss Farrow's desk.

'Looking forward to your holiday, Tom?' She gave him one of her smiles.

'Miss Farrow,' he said, avoiding her eye, 'I wanted to ask you something.'

'Yes, Tom?'

'Have you ever had a baby?'

'A baby?' She looked surprised. 'That's a strange thing to ask. You've just had a new baby, haven't you?'

'My mum has. But she's not my real mum. I'm adopted.'

'I didn't know that.'

'I thought you mightn't. My birthday's

the first of October.' He met her eye now.

Miss Farrow frowned. 'I don't quite follow, Tom.'

'I wouldn't say anything to anyone else.'

'Say what? What's on your mind? Tell me,' she said gently. 'Something is, isn't it? I've thought so for a while.'

'My real mum's name was Louise.'

She stared at him and her eyes widened. 'I see. You thought that maybe I—?'

He couldn't say anything more now. His tongue felt stuck to the roof of his mouth.

She shook her head. 'I'm sorry, Tom.'

He backed out of the room.

'Tom, wait a minute,' she said.

He didn't wait. He turned and ran. He ran all the way along the corridors and through the playground and he didn't even hear Sam shouting after him. His heart was hammering and he thought his head would explode.

When he got home he made straight for his tree. He scrambled up and climbed inside his house and fastened the door. Then he pulled the travelling rug up over his head and shut out the light.

Chapter Seven

Some time later, Mrs Watson came into the garden.

'Tom!' she called. 'Tom!'

He lifted his head and opened his window. He peered down. She was picking her way over the wet grass. Now she was standing at the bottom of the tree looking up.

'Come on down, Tom,' she said. 'I must talk to you and I can't do that standing here. Miss Farrow has just been to visit.'

Miss Farrow! He'd never be able to face her again. She would probably be laughing at him right this minute, telling all the other teachers.

'Imagine, Tom Watson thought I was his mother!'

'I don't want to come down,' he said. 'I want to stay up here. For ever and ever.'

'Don't be silly now, love! It's getting dark.'

A scream arose within the house, and then another, and another. Marigold was getting wound up. Her mother had to go back inside.

Tom ate a biscuit from his tin and listened to the birds. They were singing their good-night choruses.

A light rain began to fall. He liked the pattering sound it made on his roof. He pulled the travelling rug back round him and snuggled down. Through the window he could watch the silvery drops of rain as they landed on the branches. They held there for a moment or two, and then dropped down.

Half an hour or so later, Mrs Watson came out again. The light was fading fast. Tom could just make out her dim shape in the grey garden. She was carrying a ladder this time. She set it up against the tree.

She climbed up until she was almost level with his house.

'Come in, please, Tom, love! You can't stay there all night!'

'Yes, I can,' he said.

'Please!'

He didn't answer. His throat felt bottled up.

She sighed and went back down. She returned with a heaped plate of sandwiches and an apple and a glass of

milk and set them on the top step of the
ladder.

When she had gone he brought them
in. He realised he was hungry. He ate
all the sandwiches and drank the milk,
deciding to leave the apple until later.

He heard a meow. He opened the door
and the cat came in.

'All right, Percy, you can stay, if you behave yourself!'

Tom was pleased to see him and feel his warm body rubbing against his and Percy was only too pleased to settle down under the rug. Soon he was purring.

Tom felt sleepy himself. A yawn overcame him. His eyes closed.

He awoke at first light, feeling a little stiff but quite well rested. He opened the door and looked out at the morning. Dew glistened on the grass.

Almost immediately, the back door of

the house opened. Mrs Watson came to the foot of the tree.

'Are you coming down now, Tom?' she asked.

'No,' he said. 'I like living up here.'

'I didn't sleep all night. I sat by the kitchen window watching the garden.'

'You didn't have to,' he said.

'Yes, I did,' she said fiercely. 'I'm your mother, whether you like it or not!'

She went back inside. Tom ate his apple and drank some juice.

Percy woke up and scrambled down the tree to do his yowling act at the kitchen window. He wanted his breakfast. He was allowed in and when he came back out he spent a long time on the window sill cleaning his whiskers.

The next time the back door opened Mrs Watson emerged with the pram.

She liked to put Marigold out in the fresh air for her morning nap. She arranged the cat netting over the top of the pram and put on the brake, watched by both Percy and Tom. She didn't look at either of them. She went back inside.

Tom took one of his books from the shelf and settled down to read. He'd have liked to have had a run round the garden first but he'd have to wait till his mother went shopping.

He read for some time, lost in the world of the book. Then he yawned and stretched as best he could in the small space. His arms and legs were beginning to feel restless. He looked down, hoping she might have taken the baby to the shops and left the garden free.

But she hadn't. The pram was still there. But where was Percy? Tom opened the door of his house to get a better view. Something grey was lying underneath the white netting on the baby's pram! It was Percy! He must have managed to sneak under. Mrs Watson can't have fastened it properly.

'Percy!' yelled Tom. 'Get off!'

Percy paid no attention. He was comfortably asleep. Babies are soft and smell of milk and make nice pillows.

Tom went like a rocket down the tree, scraping his knees and screaming at Percy as he went. He raced across the grass to the pram.

He pulled off the net, grabbed the cat by the scruff of the neck and dropped him over the side.

He bent over the pram. The baby was lying on her back. He lifted her up, holding her head very carefully so that it wouldn't wobble.

'It's all right, Marigold,' he said. 'You're going to be all right.'

Her face was very flushed. But she was still breathing.

Tom let out a big sigh. He'd been terrified that Percy might have smothered her.

'What's going on, Tom?' Mrs Watson was at the back door. 'What's been happening?'

'Percy almost smothered Marigold,' he said.

'Oh, my goodness!' Mrs Watson came running to take the baby into her own arms. 'I can't have put the net on properly. How awful! Did you lift Percy off, Tom? Do you realise – you saved her life?'

'Who saved whose life?' asked a voice.

'Dad!' shouted Tom. His father had appeared round the side of the house. 'What are you doing here? Mum said you were a hundred miles away.'

'I was,' said Mr Watson. 'But when your mum rang me this morning, I jumped in the car straight away and drove here to see you.'

'I waited until this morning to phone, Tom,' said Mrs Watson. 'I thought you'd come down.'

She took the baby into the house, leaving them alone together.

'You drove all that way to see me?' said Tom.

'Of course! I was worried about you. I'd drive to the ends of the earth if you were in trouble.' Mr Watson put his hands on Tom's shoulders. 'I know how you're feeling, son. But you matter to us every bit as much as Marigold.'

'But she's your real child.'

'And you think you're not? I have to tell you that you are! Not everything comes down to being related by blood. Some parents who've given birth to their children don't love them. But we love you! Look at me, Tom! You've never doubted that, have you?'

Tom looked at Mr Watson. His unreal father. But he didn't seem unreal to him. He was his dad, after all. He flung himself into his dad's arms and they held on tightly to each other.

'Let's go inside and have some breakfast, shall we?' said his dad. 'I don't know about you but I'm starving. I drove all that way on an empty stomach.'

Marigold was lying in her basket on the kitchen counter, gurgling happily as if nothing had happened. Her mother hadn't recovered quite so quickly. She was looking white in the face.

Tom kissed her. 'I'm sorry I worried you, Mum,' he said.

'That's all right, love. Perhaps it's as well you were up in your tree house. Otherwise Marigold might really have been smothered.'

Tom went to look at the baby. She smiled at him and he smiled back. Once she stopped yowling so much and settled down she might not be so bad to have around.

He put his finger into her soft little

hand and she closed her fingers round his. Her grip was amazingly strong. Maybe she knew he'd saved her life.

'I might take her up to my tree house when she's bigger,' he said. 'But only if she doesn't yowl.'

'I think she'd like that,' said his dad. 'You are her brother, after all. And that's pretty special, isn't it?'

Tortoise Trouble

Joan Lingard

Tortoise Trouble

Joan Lingard

Robbie doesn't want to move from his home in the glen to live in a flat in the city, and he knows that neither does his tortoise, Herman.

But when Robbie's new teacher asks the class to write about their pets, his story about Herman and recent reports of tortoise thieves intrigue the other children, and Robbie begins to make friends. Then one day Herman goes missing. The work of a tortoise gang – or could the culprit be closer to home?

The Adventures of Jake
The Best Dog in the World

Annette and Nick Butterworth

Collect all five fantastic adventures featuring Jake,
the loveable scruff who can't help but get into
mischief . . .

Rita the Rescuer and Other Stories
Hilda Offen

Rita is the youngest in her family and she's forever

being left out for being 'too young'. But she has a

secret identity and when she changes into her rescuer

outfit, nothing can stop her from saving the day…

In this 3-in-1 edition, see Rita discover her

rescuer outfit and then embark on a series of

heroic adventures and daring rescues that include

encountering a haunted house and taking on a

mermaid-eating sea monster.

You can find out more about Joan Lingard's books
and other Catnip titles by visiting
www.catnippublishing.co.uk